Lulu
and the Duck in the Park

Look out for more books by

Hilary McKay

Charlie and the Cat Flap
Charlie and the Great Escape
Charlie and the Big Snow
Charlie and the Rocket Boy
Charlie and the Cheese and Onion Crisps
Charlie and the Haunted Tent
Charlie and the Tooth Fairy
Charlie and the Big Birthday Bash

www.hilarymckay.co.uk

Lulu
and the Duck in the Park

Hilary Mckay

Illustrated by Priscilla Lamont

MSCHOLASTIC

First published in the UK in 2011 by Scholastic Children's Books
An imprint of Scholastic Ltd
Euston House, 24 Eversholt Street
London, NW1 1DB, UK
Registered office: Westfield Road, Southam, Warwickshire, CV47 0RA
SCHOLASTIC and associated logos are trademarks and/or
registered trademarks of Scholastic Inc.

ISBN 978 1 407 11737 9

A CIP catalogue record for this book is available
from the British Library.

Typeset by M Rules
Printed by CPI Bookmarque, Croydon, CR0 4TD

Papers used by Scholastic Children's Books are made from
wood grown in sustainable forests.

1 3 5 7 9 10 8 6 4 2

www.scholastic.co.uk/zone

Chapter One
Lulu and Mellie

Lulu was famous for animals. Her famousness for animals was known throughout the whole neighbourhood.

Animals mattered more to Lulu than anything else in the world. All animals, from the sponsored polar bear family that had been her best Christmas present, to the hairiest unwanted spider in the school cloakroom.

Lulu loved them all. She was always rescuing and comforting and carrying animals home.

Lulu might have been famous for other things, such as the way she ate apples, which left no apple at all, except the stalk and the pips.

Or for jumping off swings, right at the highest point of the swing. (Swing jumping was a bad and dangerous habit of Lulu's which caused her many sore hands and banged knees.)

"Mad!" said Lulu's cousin Mellie when Lulu jumped off swings. It was usually

Lulu did not just clean them out. She played with them and talked to them. She exercised them and fed them. She looked them up in library books and googled them on the internet. She thought about them.

"What would I want," wondered Lulu, "if I was a hamster in a cage? A spider in a bath? The Class 3 guinea pig?"

Lulu's hamster had cardboard mazes to explore, and surprise parcels of nuts to unwrap. The spiders in Lulu's house had a little rope ladder to help them out of the bath. The Class 3 guinea pig went home with Lulu for holidays and had a wonderful time going on outings to the park.

"Thank goodness I don't have to take him home," said Mrs Holiday, Lulu's class teacher (famous for her biscuit tin of exotic biscuits, and her icy blue glares).

"*Mrs Holiday!*" said Lulu, shocked. "He's an amazing guinea pig! For a guinea pig."

"I'm sure he is," agreed Mrs Holiday. "But I am not a guinea pig sort of person. In fact," added Mrs Holiday, "I could manage quite happily with no guinea pigs at all."

When the Class 3 guinea pig was more annoying than usual (his bathroom habits were awful and he chewed up anything leaning against his cage), Mrs Holiday would glare at him and say, "Hmmm!"

"Don't you like animals, Mrs Holiday?" Lulu asked once.

"I like animals," said Mrs Holiday, "in the wild. Perfectly happy, but a long way off!"

Lulu agreed about the animals being perfectly happy. That was good. But she did not agree about them being a long way off. *The closer the better*, Lulu thought.

"Perhaps you don't know many animals," she suggested to Mrs Holiday.

"Hardly any," said Mrs Holiday cheerfully.

Lulu tried to help with that.

She thought of lots of ways.

Mrs Holiday would not be helped. She said, "No, no, no, absolutely not," when Lulu offered to organize a pet show for the school summer fair.

"I'm not sure I want to look!" she said, when Lulu brought in photographs of the Snail World she had built at the end of her garden. "Snails are just not me, Lulu! In fact, I'm afraid I don't like them much at all."

"It's not just snails," said Lulu. "Slugs too!"

"Even worse!" cried Mrs Holiday.

Lulu bought a packet of dog treats, and a few days later her old dog Sam cleverly trailed her all the way to school.

Mrs Holiday was not a bit pleased about that. Lulu was allowed to give him a drink of water, but after his drink Sam had to go to the caretaker's room and be tied up till home time.

"Can't he stay with me?" begged Lulu.

"Certainly not," said Mrs Holiday.

"He would be so good! You'd not even notice him!"

"I am noticing him already!" said Mrs Holiday, glaring icy blue glares at Sam, who was panting round the classroom, banging into things.

"He's a very nice dog," said Lulu pleadingly. "Look how friendly he is!"

Sam was now snuffling like a vacuum cleaner at the guinea pig cage. His

snuffling made the guinea pig squeak and charge around spilling wood shavings out through the bars.

"Woof!" said Sam, loudly and happily.

"Lulu!" said Mrs Holiday, handing Lulu a skipping rope that she had cleverly knotted to make a collar and lead.

"Please take that very nice dog away AT ONCE and ask the caretaker to keep him until home time."

"Now?" asked Lulu.

"This instant!" said Mrs Holiday. "And while you are there, please borrow a dustpan and brush!"

So Lulu very slowly led Sam away, and when she came back the guinea pig was a lot calmer, and so was Mrs Holiday. Until Lulu, busily sweeping, remarked, "I think the poor guinea pig needs a friend. I have some black and white mice. If you like I could bring them in to visit him. And I expect lots of the others have pets they could bring in too."

She was right. They did. They all offered at once to bring friends for the guinea pig. Class 3 bounced in their seats in their eagerness to describe the friendliness of rats and lizards, cats and fish, terrapins and tame(ish) beetles.

"No, no, no!" exclaimed Mrs Holiday, and called an emergency meeting for Class 3. And at the meeting she explained to everyone very carefully and plainly that if the Class 3 guinea pig ever had a single friend brought in to visit . . . any sort of friend, a snaily friend or a whiskery friend, a very large friend like Sammy, or a very small friend, like a black and white mouse, then the Class 3 guinea pig would unfortunately have to leave Class 3 for ever.

"But where would he go?" asked Lulu.

"*We would swop him for the Class 2 stick insects!*" said Mrs Holiday. "Class 2 would be very pleased to swop," she continued, ignoring the howls and groans all around her, "and I should not mind a bit. I much prefer quiet unsmelly stick insects to squeaky rowdy guinea pigs. So. You have been warned!"

Class 3 were silent with shock.

They all gazed at the guinea pig and thought how gloomy things would be without him. No more cheerful noisy interruptions of squeaks in quiet lessons.

No more guinea-pig food to chew in hungry moments. No more useful sausage-shaped guinea-pig poos to flick around the classroom.

At the end of the afternoon everyone grumbled at Lulu, for making Mrs Holiday think of such an awful idea.

They grumbled a lot, and the one who grumbled most of all was Mellie.

"Mrs Holiday really meant it," said Mellie, as she and Lulu swung in the little park together on their way home from school that day. "She would swop, I'm sure she would. And just looking at those stick insects makes me feel itchy all over. I think I may be allergic to them actually. So. . ."

There was a very long, swinging Mellie-style silence.

"I suppose I'd have to change schools," said Mellie.

"Oh," shouted Lulu. "What a fuss!" And she swallowed the last of the apple she was eating, stuffed the stalks and pips in her pocket, jumped at the highest point of the swing and after a wonderful, but very brief, time flying through the air, landed with a *smash*.

Then she gathered up Sam's skipping-rope lead, and hobbled away.

So Mellie, who was to have tea with Lulu that day, stopped her swing by scraping her toes on the ground, and ran after her (leaving her school jumper hanging forgotten on the climbing frame).

They walked back to Lulu's house, arguing.

Lulu said it was not fair that the poor guinea pig had to live all alone with no friendly visitors.

Mellie said it was not fair if Lulu made Mrs Holiday so cross that he had to be swopped for the Class 2 stick insects.

Lulu made a list of all the quiet, peaceful animals she could bring to school that Mrs Holiday would never notice. Mellie got crosser and crosser. The animals on the list got bigger and less quiet, just to annoy Mellie.

They did annoy Mellie.

"You just dare!" she said, when Lulu said rabbits in a rucksack would never be noticed.

"Anyway, it would be cruel to the rabbits," said Mellie.

"Not at all," said Lulu. "They could wear school jumpers and bounce around the play—"

"*Lulu!*" wailed Mellie.

"What?"

"Where's my jumper? My jumper's gone! Didn't I have it when I came out of school? Didn't I? I did! I know I did!"

"You must have left it by the swings," said Lulu, and they ran back together to see.

It was gone.

Mellie's things were always gone.

Mellie tipped her school bag upside down on the pavement to see if her jumper could possibly, magically, be at the bottom. Pencils and pens rolled everywhere and disappeared. A pound coin spun neatly on its edge for a moment and vanished down a drain.

Mellie sat down in the middle of the muddle and wailed, "It's all your fault, Lulu!"

She hated losing things.

Lulu collected books and pencils, hairclips, water bottles, homework sheets and crumbled biscuits. Sam licked Mellie's face, enjoying the taste of tears.

"I wouldn't have lost it if I hadn't been worrying about stick insects," said Mellie, sniffing and feeding Sam biscuit crumbs while Lulu repacked her bag for her. "I just DON'T like stick insects!"

"Well, we won't have stick insects!" said Lulu, kindly. "You can stop worrying. I won't bring visitors for the guinea pig, and Mrs Holiday won't get mad and . . . *I know what will cheer you up!*"

Lulu scrambled out of her school jumper, chewed off the name tag with

her teeth, shook it out and pulled it over
Mellie's head.

"I've got another one at home," she
said.

Chapter Two
Morning in the Park

Tuesday was Class 3's favourite day at school.

This was because Tuesday was swimming day.

The big swimming pool in the centre of town was so close to school that Class 3 did not have to take a bus to get there, like other schools did. They could get there in a few minutes by walking.

First thing every Tuesday morning, Class 3 walked down the hill from school,

 21

around the narrow cobbled streets by the church, and across the town park to the pool.

The town park was wonderful. Twenty times bigger than the little playing-field park where Mellie and Lulu swung after school.

It had huge trees and grassy slopes and twisting paths.

It had a climbing wall and a giant slide.

It had a sweet shop and a life-sized pirate ship becalmed in a sea of bark.

It had a lake with two little islands and a hundred noisy ducks.

Getting Class 3 past the climbing wall without anyone climbing, and the sweet shop without anyone darting in, and the lake without anyone getting wet, was the hardest part of Mrs Holiday's week.

Getting them back to school again, wet-haired, starving and weighed down by soggy swimming bags, was nearly impossible.

Mrs Holiday didn't even try.

On Tuesday mornings after swimming, Mrs Holiday marched Class 3 to the bandstand by the lake. In the bandstand bags were dropped, boxes were opened and Class 3 ate their shivery bites.

That was what Mrs Holiday, who had been brought up in Scotland, called the biscuity, appley, peanut-butter-sandwichy snack that came after swimming.

A shivery bite.

Mrs Holiday was quite old. She had taught many, many classes of children. Some of them were grown up now, with families of their own. The things they had learnt at school, the Romans and the Vikings, the way a bean grows in a jam jar, how to carry an egg on a spoon, and the names of the planets, had faded from their minds.

But none of them ever forgot their shivery bites.

After the shivery bites were eaten, Lulu and Mellie and the rest of Class 3 were allowed ten minutes to climb aboard the pirate ship, or slide down the giant slide, or get stuck on the climbing wall. Lulu always saved the end of her shivery bite for her favourite duck. It was a brown one, with one white wing.

The white-winged duck had a nest under the bushes on the bank by the path. It was so tame it let Lulu come right up to visit.

"I should like a duck," Lulu often remarked.

For Class 3, that ten minutes in the town park was the best part of the whole cheerful morning. After it was over they went back to school and were good for a week so that they could do it all again after the next swimming lesson.

That was what usually happened on Tuesdays.

But this Tuesday was different.
This Tuesday – the day after Lulu's dog Sam trailed Lulu to school and Mellie lost her jumper and Class 3 learnt the very real danger of their guinea pig being swopped for a box of stick insects – the day after all that happened, things were very different and terrible in the park.

It was early spring. Every tree was exploding like a firework with bright green leaves. Every flower bed blazed with tulips and daffodils. And every one of the hundred ducks that lived by the lake had a nest of eggs, or newly hatched ducklings. The white-winged duck was not the only one to make her nest among the bushes by the path. There was a whole line of them. "Duck Street", the park keepers called it.

There was a fine view of Duck Street from the bandstand.

Class 3 had just unpacked their shivery bites when the trouble began. The park was suddenly filled with noise. Shouting and barking and running footsteps. The splashings and quackings of a hundred frightened ducks.

Two enormous dogs came tearing across the park towards Duck Street. Two heavy black dogs with thick leather collars. They were chasing the ducks, and chasing each other, and snarling and snapping. Flower beds were flattened. Ducks squawked in

panic and beat their wings. Ducklings fluttered and cheeped. And all along the Duck Street, under the new green bushes, nests were trodden on and scattered and smashed.

"NO!" screeched Lulu, and ran to try and rescue her white-winged duck.

"No!" cried Mrs Holiday, and grabbed her just in time.

So Lulu had to watch.

For a long, long time no one could catch those terrible dogs. Not their owner with his two empty leads, nor the park keepers who came running from every direction.

Those dogs were wild. And they ran so fast, and they appeared so suddenly in so many unexpected places, that it seemed like there were far more than two.

"Keep those kids in the bandstand!" a park keeper yelled at Mrs Holiday, and she did. She stood at the top of the bandstand steps like a soldier on guard.

Class 3 were screaming and pointing and shouting, and some of them were crying.

"Class 3, be silent, please!" commanded Mrs Holiday.

Class 3 became silent.

Then Mrs Holiday took the register, calling each person's name in turn, just like she did every morning at school. All through the register she stood at the top of the steps, guarding the open entrance of the bandstand.

Now the bandstand was the quietest place in the park, but all around still the dogs ran wild.

One of them ran right up the bandstand steps.

"SIT!!!" bellowed Mrs Holiday in a voice that no one in Class 3 ever guessed she possessed.

A miracle happened.

Right in front of Mrs Holiday, right under her icy blue glare, the dog sat down.

His owner was there in a moment.

And two seconds later he was back on his chain.

The second dog did not even have to be told. He slunk towards the other with his tail between his legs.

Class 3 yelled and cheered and clapped their heroic Mrs Holiday, and as rapidly as they had arrived, the dogs vanished.

But the park was wrecked, and Duck Street was tragic.

Terrified ducks, huddled on the islands.

Lost ducklings.

Ruined nests.

Smashed and sticky eggs.

Class 3, walking two by two along the path by the lake, stepped carefully to avoid the scattered leaves and feathers of trodden nests. They tried not to look at the broken shells.

Lulu and Mellie were the last to leave the bandstand.

Mellie was still frightened. She looked anxiously behind them all the time, half expecting to see another huge dog exploding from the bushes.

She didn't see what Lulu saw.

There was not one unhurt nest left in Duck Street. The white-winged duck and her neighbours were all gone. But from the place where the white-winged duck had built her nest, something was rolling down the grassy bank.

A last blue egg from the Duck Street nests, the only one that hadn't been broken.

Faster and faster it rolled.

Any moment it would smash on the path.

34

Before Mellie turned around, before anyone saw, before she even thought what she was doing, Lulu had caught it up and put it in her pocket.

It was still warm.

Chapter Three
Life with an Egg

Lulu's hand curled round the egg in her fleecy jacket pocket, enjoying its polished roundness. It was not quite perfect, she discovered. There was faint zigzag crack, so fine her fingers found it and lost it and found it again. There was a rough patch at one end, where a fragment of shell was missing.

Well, thought Lulu, *it's had a terrible time, this egg! Of course there are bumps. A few bumps don't matter. Anyway, now it is safe.*

That was what Lulu thought. Nothing sensible, such as *What am I going to do with this egg?* Or scary, such as, *What am I going to do with this egg if it smashes?*

She just plodded along beside Mellie and thought, *Safe.*

Mellie was also thinking. Not one thought, like Lulu. Lots of thoughts, barging into her brain from all directions.

I wish I had a tissue, Mellie thought. *A handkerchief. A paper towel. Something for my nose. It's the cold and swimming pool water making it run.*

Not crying.

Those dogs!

Those dogs should be arrested. Can you arrest dogs? Would they understand? They understood Mrs Holiday when she said "Sit!"

Mrs Holiday was . . . was . . . was. . .

Titanic! thought Mellie, and skipped to

have found the perfect word.

She skipped straight into the backs of Charlie and Henry, who were walking in front.

Henry (who always fell over at the smallest push) toppled right under her feet. Mellie tripped and fell on top of him, grabbing Lulu on the way down.

Lulu landed all curled up, wrapped around like a hedgehog with its paws in its pockets.

My egg! My egg! she thought, hardly daring to move for fear of what she might discover.

Mellie and Henry scrambled to their feet, blaming each other.

Charlie began a slow-motion action replay for anyone who had missed seeing the fun first time round.

Mrs Holiday came hurrying down the line of children, crying, "Everybody, quiet! Up you get, Lulu! Take my hand!"

Lulu, who was busy very slowly and carefully uncurling from around the egg, said, "No, no! Don't touch me! Leave me alone!"

"Are you hurt?" asked Mrs Holiday, astonished at such rudeness.

Lulu didn't even hear her. Her fingers were exploring her pocket for damage. Was the egg broken? How broken? Fatally broken?

"Come on, Lulu!" said Mellie, tugging her arm impatiently, and looked shocked when Lulu pushed her away.

"Mellie was trying to help you!" snapped Mrs Holiday, her eyes blue and icy.

Lulu, on her feet at last, gave a great sigh. Not broken. Wonderful.

"Sorry, Mellie," she said.

Mrs Holiday was still cross.

"You can walk the rest of the way back to school with me!" she told Lulu. "Stand up properly, please, and take your hands out of your pockets . . . *goodness, Charlie!*"

Charlie's nose was the sort that bleeds at the smallest excuse. Now a mixture of cold and swimming and excitement had started it again.

Blood was streaming down his face and splattering the pavement. Charlie, who always enjoyed the shrieks and fuss that went with nosebleeds, was bouncing with pleasure.

"I'm a vampire!" he called happily,
diving for Henry's throat.

So in the end it was Charlie who
had to walk with Mrs Holiday, with his
swimming towel clutched to his nose,
while Lulu and Mellie tagged along
behind.

Every few minutes Mrs Holiday glared
over her shoulder at Lulu to make sure

she knew she was still in trouble. Every few minutes Lulu looked unhappily down at the ground to show that she did.

Everyone was very relieved to get back to school.

Mrs Holiday made a speech in the playground.

"It was a difficult morning for all of us," she said. "Difficult – Henry and Charlie, come and stand over here! Right beside me! One each side! How *very* silly! – Difficult and quite upsetting. I know we were all sad to see what happened in the park – Lulu, you look like you are trying to put your head in your pocket. It would be nice if you listened! – Now, Class 3! What have we learnt to do after times like this? Do you remember? Yes, Mellie? Good girl!"

"Everyone should take handkerchiefs

if they are going swimming," said Mellie. "Because afterwards the water runs out of your nose."

"Not quite what I was thinking of," said Mrs Holiday, "but a sensible idea. I was hoping you would say we *learn* . . . what do we learn?"

"Shout 'Sit!' at mad dogs?" suggested someone.

"We *learn* that pets are a great responsibility," said Mrs Holiday. "Isn't that true, Lulu?"

Lulu jumped guiltily.

"And when we have *learnt*," continued Mrs Holiday, "*we leave it behind* because . . . who wants to explain?"

"Because the ducks are all dead," said Henry.

"Because worrying does not change anything," said Mrs Holiday. "(The ducks

44

are not all dead. They may even lay again.) We learn, leave it behind, and move on to make things better!"

That was what Mrs Holiday always said after any awful event. The time the Class 3 play for parents turned into a battle. The afternoon the Class 3 football team lost ten nil to Class 2. The day the Dinner Lady Trick went wrong.

"How can we make this better?" enquired Mrs Holiday now.

Class 3 thought of lots of ways. Duck food to cheer up the ducks. A poster for the park saying, PLEASE KEEP DOGS ON LEADS. Zappers

for park keepers
so that they could
zap mad dogs.
Zappers for ducks
so they could do it
themselves.

Lulu thought of
her egg, and said
nothing.

"Lots of good
ideas!" said Mrs
Holiday. "And
some not quite
so good. Charlie, you will make it start
again, doing that! There, you have done!
Come here! And the rest of you, jackets
off and reading books out while I look
at Charlie's nose."

Class 3 streamed away to the
cloakroom. Lulu followed last of all. She

had forgotten she would have to take her jacket off when she got back to school.

Thank goodness for Charlie's nose, she thought, as she waited for the others to leave the cloakroom. It would keep Mrs Holiday busy for a few minutes while she, Lulu, took off her jacket and found a safe place to keep a large blue egg in a pocketless jumper.

Up the sleeves? Impossible.

Inside the front? Far too loose.

How on earth do ducks manage, wondered Lulu, and answered the question herself a moment later: *nests*.

Lulu did not have a nest, but there were plenty of woolly hats lying around by the coat pegs. Lulu borrowed two, and made a hat nest, with one hat inside the other and the egg warm in the middle.

The egg looked much safer in its hat nest.

Now what? wondered Lulu. *What do ducks do with their nests?*

They sat on them.

Lulu could not sit on her nest, but she did the next best thing. She stuffed it under her jumper.

Does it show? wondered Lulu, looking at her dim reflection in the glass of the cloakroom door.

It did, but not terribly. And Mrs Holiday, Lulu was very glad to see, was still busy with Charlie.

So, feeling rather like a duck herself, Lulu waddled back to the classroom and sat down at the table she shared with Mellie.

Mellie had noticed.

"What have you got stuffed under your jumper?" she demanded.

"Under my jumper?"

"There's definitely something! Tell me! I won't tell."

"Well. A hat."

"A *hat*?"

"Yes."

"*Why?*"

"To keep it safe," replied Lulu, after some thought.

"Safe from what?"

"Getting lost."

"Oh," said Mellie in a rather surprised voice, and then "Oh!" again, in a rather impressed voice. *That isn't such a bad idea,* she thought. She might try it herself.

Maybe she would not lose so many things, if she kept them stuffed safely under her jumper.

The only problem was:

"I lost my jumper," said Mellie, out loud. "This one I'm wearing is yours. Too tight for stuffing much under. OW!"

Mellie, experimenting with her pencil case, had stabbed herself with her ruler. That made Mrs Holiday look across and say, "Mellie, please put your pencil case back on the table. It is time we all did some work. Everyone sit down! Charlie, hold that ice pack on your *nose*! It will never work there!"

"He doesn't want it to work," remarked Henry.

"Of course he does!" said Mrs Holiday. "And anyway, all good things come to an end. Bloodletting is over. This is now maths. Who can remember what we were thinking about yesterday?"

Nobody could.

"Perimeters!" said Mrs Holiday, writing the word on the board. "And where would we find a perimeter? You all knew yesterday!"

Class 3 shook their heads. What they knew on one day had nothing to do with what they remembered the next.

 51

"A perimeter," said Mrs Holiday, "is a line that goes round the edge. A perimeter of a circle goes all around the edge of the circle. A perimeter of a field would go. . . Where would it go? Tell me, Henry!"

"In the grass," said Henry.

"All round the edge of the field," said Mrs Holiday.

"That would be in the grass," said Henry. "Like I said."

"Today," continued Mrs Holiday, ignoring Henry, "we are going to *measure* some perimeters! How could we measure a perimeter?"

"Is it a trick question?" enquired Mellie.

"No, it is a perfectly sensible question," said Mrs Holiday patiently. "Lulu, why are you holding your front like that? Is everything all right?"

Lulu nodded, and said, "Yes, thank you Mrs Holiday", although she was not quite certain that was true. A minute before, the hat nest had suddenly seemed to move. To shake, like a tummy rumble. Just for a moment. Perhaps it had been a tummy rumble.

"Good," said Mrs Holiday, gathering up a pile of what looked like junk from the lost property cupboard. "Now, we are going to investigate the perimeters of all these shapes. Working in pairs . . . there's a fan for you, Charlie and Henry! You girls can take these leaves. Who deserves the angel wings, I wonder?"

Up and down the classroom walked Mrs Holiday, giving out strange objects to pairs of people. A enormous painted fan. A circle of curly cabbage leaves. A pair of cardboard angel's wings, a parasol, a pair of gloves, a T-shirt and a kite.

"All these things have perimeters," she said "This baby suit. This rather lovely peacock feather. . . You take that, Dan. . . On my table are pens and tape measures and all sizes of paper. First you must *estimate* (an estimate is a sensible guess, remember!) the perimeter of the object that I have given you, and then you must *measure* it. . . Think hard how you will do that! Lulu and Mellie. . ."

She paused at their table. They were the last pair left without a shape to investigate, and her hands were empty.

"The perimeter of a person," she said. "Lulu, I think! Now then, Mellie! How will you investigate the perimeter of Lulu?"

"I know! I know!" said Mellie, rushing to the table to collect the largest piece of paper and the juiciest fat felt-tip pen. "I know, I know, I know, don't tell me!"

Mellie spread her piece of paper in the middle of the classroom floor and pulled the top off of her pen.

"Lie down, Lulu!" she ordered.

"*Mellie!*" moaned Lulu. "*Lie down there? Now?*"

"Not now," said Mrs Holiday, passing on to another group of investigators. "First you must estimate. Don't forget that!"

"First!" hissed Lulu. "You must listen, Mellie! I can't lie down there."

"You've got to," said Mellie, testing her

55

green felt-tip pen on her arm. "Soon as we've estimated. I estimate three metres. One and a half up one side and over your head. One and a half down the other side and round your feet. Three. Now lie down!"

"Mellie, listen!" said Lulu. "Stop jumping about and listen! It's not just a hat up my jumper. It's two hats. . ."

"Take 'em out!" said Mellie, waving her pen.

"And an egg."

"An *egg*?"

"A duck egg. From the park."

Mellie stared.

"It's still warm."

Mellie's eyes grew rounder and rounder.

"And I think . . . I think I felt it move!"

Mellie got the giggles of the most painful silent sort and lay on her front weeping and gasping.

"It musn't get broken," hissed Lulu, shaking her, "because then there would be a duckling. A duckling! Here in this classroom! And you know what Mrs Holiday said yesterday about no more animals!"

"Oh," said Mellie, suddenly becoming calm. "Not good."

She looked across the room at the guinea pig who might so easily be swopped for stick insects.

And then Mellie became wonderful.

In no time the piece of paper for Lulu to lie on was whisked to the Reading Corner, the most private place in the classroom. Then, in one green juicy line, Mellie drew all around the edge of her friend. Before anyone had noticed anything unusual about Lulu's jumper at all they were back at the table again and marking off the perimeter of a person in neat green centimetres.

"Exactly what I hoped you would do," said Mrs Holiday, when she came to see how they were getting on.

"Eggsactly!" whispered Mellie, when she

had gone, and gave one of her sudden
snorts of laughter. "Is it still safe?"

"I think so. I hope so. If I can just
keep it not broken until after school.
Then I'm going ask Mum to let me take
it to the vet."

"Yes, he'll know how to hatch it,"
agreed Mellie. "And then you'll have a
duckling. Lucky thing!"

"I'll share."

"It will need a pond."

"How hard is it to dig a pond?" asked
Lulu.

"I'll help," said Mellie.

Lulu became much happier. Life with
a hat nest under her jumper was much
easier with a friend who understood.
Mellie was very useful. When things
needed fetching or picking up or holding,
she was there to help. At lunchtime she

was a human shield that stopped the hat nest being squashed in the lunchtime queue. After lunch, when the rest of the school were charging round the playground, she visited the library and found a book on ducks.

The book made Lulu and Mellie rather sad.

Mother ducks, it said, talked to their ducklings before they were even hatched.

"They talk to their *eggs*?" asked Mellie, astonished.

"And the ducklings inside the eggs learn the sound of their mothers' voices," read Lulu. "And the ducklings talk back to their mothers! Oh my poor white-winged duck!"

"I don't think that can be true," said Mellie. "I don't see how anything could make a sound in an egg!"

"Just in case," said Lulu, worrying, "I should quack to this egg. So it doesn't get lonely."

"Should I quack too?" asked Mellie. "Would it help?"

Lulu said she thought that would help a lot, and it did. She felt much less silly quacking with a friend than quacking alone.

After lunch came music. That was
difficult. Class 3 were practising a song for
the Easter play, with singers and recorders.
Mellie's recorder had been lost months
before, but Lulu still had hers. There was
no possible excuse that could save her
from having to stand in front of the class
with the rest of the recorder group and
play her recorder.

"I'll take care of the egg," said Mellie
bravely, and she did. For the next half

hour she cradled the hat nest in her hands under the table, hardly daring to breathe.

Music passed safely.

The day that had begun in such a fuss of water and dogs and quacking and tears became more and more peaceful. Mrs Holiday handed out doodling paper and picked up a new storybook.

"*Harry Potter,*" she read, "*and the Philosopher's Stone.*"

She had been promising to begin it for weeks.

CRACK!

Even through two hats and her school shirt, Lulu felt that crack.

Chapter Four
Life With A Duck

Lulu looked across at Mellie to see if she had noticed anything. Mellie was in a Mellie-dream, tilting her chair backwards, listening to the story, while she drew owls and ducks and lightning-shaped scars.

Maybe I imagined it, thought Lulu, and began very carefully to move her hand under her jumper, over the rim of the hat nest, down towards the egg.

Something?

Nothing?

Lulu jumped with shock.

No more smooth egg. Fragments of shell.

No more warm stillness. A fluttering struggle for freedom. No more quiet. A thin, high voice.

"Weep!" wheezed the front of Lulu's jumper.

"Weep!"

"Is someone being silly?" demanded Mrs Holiday, looking up from her book.

Luckily for Lulu, several people were being silly. Charlie and Henry were thumb wrestling. Someone else was having a tug of war with the guinea pig over a spelling list. Mellie fell off her chair.

Mrs Holiday snapped *Harry Potter* shut.

"Oh, Mrs Holiday!" groaned Class 3.

"*If* you would like me to read any more," said Mrs Holiday, glaring, "you will become instantly quiet and sensible. *If* you would not like me to read any more then we will spend the time on mental maths!"

Class 3 became instantly quiet and sensible. Mrs Holiday began reading once more. Lulu wrote IT'S HATCHING on her doodling paper, nudged Mellie, and pointed.

Mellie stared.

NOW? she wrote.

Lulu nodded.

DID YOU BUMP IT?

"No," whispered Lulu.

ON ITS OWN?

"Yes."

"I didn't know they did," whispered Mellie. "Not on their own! From the inside. I thought the mother duck helped them break their way out."

"Mellie!" exclaimed Mrs Holiday. "Collect your things together and come and sit by me!"

Mellie did. But not before she had scrawled on her doodling paper: WONTITSUFFKET and pushed the paper towards Lulu.

Wontitsuffket, read Lulu, puzzled. *Wontitsuffket? What is wontitsuffket?*

She looked at Mellie.

Mellie looked desperately back.

Won, read Lulu again. *Or Wont? Wont it? Wont it suffket.*

OH!

Won't it suffocate?

68

"Please Mrs Holiday," begged Lulu, "may I leave the room? Now? Quick?"

Mrs Holiday nodded, and then noticed Lulu's hands holding the front of her jumper and said, "Yes, you may. Now! Quickly! Mellie, go with her. Come back for me if Lulu is not well."

"Hurry!" added Mrs Holiday urgently, because if there was one thing she could not bear it was people being ill in her classroom.

Lulu and Mellie hurried. They raced along the corridor, burst into the empty bathroom, thankfully shut the door and leaned on it.

"Get it out! Get it out!" begged Mellie.

Lulu was already doing that. Her jumper was off. The hat nest was in her hand. She was turning back the rim. "Weep!" called the occupant suddenly. "Weep! Weep! Weep!"

There it was; a duckling. A fluffy head, already dry. Two questioning, shining black eyes. Two stumpy wings, fluttering in the sudden light. The rest still hidden in the shell.

"Weep!" called the duckling, a dry, thirsty call.

"It really is!" said Mellie. "It really, really is a real proper duckling!"

"*Weep*," insisted the duckling.

"What does it want?"

"Could it want a drink?" wondered Lulu. She wet her finger and held it so that a drop of warm water touched the duckling's beak.

"Weep!" it said, and swallowed the drop, and then another and another and fluttered with sudden energy, and stepped out of its shell.

Lulu and Mellie forgot the classroom. They forgot Mrs Holiday and *Harry Potter*. They forgot the guinea pig and the park. They sat on the cold bathroom floor with the hat nest between them and for a long time all they said was: "Look!" and "Oh!" and "Did you see that?"

In the classroom Mrs Holiday was having a hard time. Class 3 said she was not reading *Harry Potter* properly. They knew this was true because they had all seen the film. They kept putting up their hands to complain, saying things like:

"Are you skipping bits, Miss?" and, "She's not skipping bits, she's putting extra bits in" and, "When will we get to the train?" and, "My mum read it to me and there was nothing about drills" and, "Hagrid didn't talk like that!"

It seemed to poor Mrs Holiday that every time she looked up dozens of hands were waving in the air. Each hand was attached to a complaining listener.

"If you would like me to read you a book that has not been made into a film, I can do that very easily," said Mrs Holiday at last, and picked up *Key Stage 2 Mental Maths.*

The waving hands vanished and Harry Potter's adventures continued. But after a while the questions began again.

"Is this book true?" and, "Miss, can you do magic?" and, "I've never seen an owl."

"*I've* never seen a rat."

"I've never seen a *toad.*"

"I've never seen an owl, or a rat, or a toad!"

"Hands down!" roared Mrs Holiday, unable to bear one second more. "Yes, you too, Henry! Whatever it is, I don't want to know!"

So Henry sat quietly and did not tell her that the guinea pig was out until it actually vanished, along the window sill and out of the window.

That was why it wasn't for ages, not until the guinea pig was tracked down and recaptured, and the window closed, and everyone sitting quietly on their hands doing mental maths, that Mrs Holiday remembered Lulu and Mellie.

"We must go back to class," Mellie was saying to Lulu. "I must anyway, otherwise Mrs Holiday will think you are ill. I'm surprised she hasn't remem—"

That was when Mrs Holiday charged into the bathroom.

Chapter Five
Afternoon in the Park

Mrs Holiday stood in the bathroom doorway and looked down at Lulu and Mellie and the duckling, all together on the bathroom floor, and her mouth opened and closed and opened and closed like a duck that had lost its quack.

"Lulu!" she said at last.

"Mrs Holiday," said Lulu earnestly. "I didn't bring this duckling to school. I didn't bring any animal to school. I promise I didn't."

"Please don't swop the guinea pig for those awful stick insects," pleaded Mellie.

"It was only an egg when I picked it up," explained Lulu. "You can't call an egg an animal."

"Lots of people bring eggs to school," pointed out Mellie. "Packed lunches."

"Weep!" said the duckling.

"It rolled out from the bush where the white-winged duck had her nest," said Lulu. "I picked it up just before it smashed on the path. All the other eggs were broken.

I was going to take it to the vet."

"Oh, Lulu," said Mrs Holiday, sighing.

"She made it a hat nest to keep it safe," said Mellie. "But it hatched anyway."

"*Where* did it hatch?" asked Mrs Holiday.

"Under my jumper," said Lulu.

"Lulu," said Mrs Holiday, "I have been teaching in schools for twenty-seven years. In all those twenty-seven years, no one has ever hatched a duckling under their jumper. . ."

Mrs Holiday paused to take a very clean folded handkerchief out from her pocket. She dabbed it carefully at the corner of each of her eyes.

". . .as far as I know," said Mrs Holiday, and dabbed her eyes again.

Was she laughing, or was she crying? Lulu and Mellie could not tell.

79

"Well," said Mrs Holiday, putting her handkerchief away and becoming her old bossy self again. "This is no place for a duckling. It belongs in the park. Maybe . . . maybe. . . You girls wait here!"

With that she was gone, and Lulu and Mellie were left staring at each other.

"Was she angry?" wondered Lulu, but Mellie shook her head and said she did not know.

The duckling was crying again. "Weep, weep."

A lost, unhappy sound.

Lulu looked around the room. She saw bright, shabby paint and the underside of sinks. Waste pipes and tiles. A notice on the door: DON'T FORGET TO WASH YOUR HANDS!

Mrs Holiday is right, Lulu thought. *This is no place for a duckling.*

She was still thinking this when Mrs Holiday came back. She was carrying a box and she was in a great rush.

"We have twenty-five minutes until the bell goes," she told Lulu and Mellie. "Hurry up! The secretary has very kindly agreed to stay with Class 3 (Heaven help her). Get your jackets, girls, and we will go back to the park. Perhaps we can find the duck with the white wing and give her back her duckling again."

In no time the duckling was rushed into the box.

The secretary was given Mrs Holiday's exotic biscuit tin to use as a last resort.

And then Lulu and Mellie and Mrs Holiday set off to find the duck with the white wing, in spring sunshine that felt as warm as summer.

The park was as quiet as if nothing had happened. The paths were swept clean of spoiled nests and broken shells. The flower beds were tidy again. No huge silly dogs tore through the bushes. No children

squealed in the bandstand. On the lake
the ducks were almost silent. Some of
them slept on the little islands, one eye
open, one leg tucked up. Little chains of
ducklings looped in and out of the reeds
at the edge.

"Measuring the perimeter," said Mellie.

But on the bank by the bandstand a
brown duck with a white wing searched
among the bushes. Searched and searched,
and called and called.

"Weep!
Weep!" cried
the duckling
from the
box in Lulu's
hand.

The duck with the white wing paused.

"Listening," whispered Mellie. "Hurry,
Lulu!"

So Lulu lifted the duckling from the hat nest and tucked him back under the bushes where he had lived so long as an egg.

He was hardly alone for a moment.

Lulu and Mellie and Mrs Holiday sighed great sighs of happiness and relief, and went back to school, just in time for the bell to go home.

"What a day!" groaned Mrs Holiday, collapsed like a rag doll in a staffroom chair. "What a day, what a day!"

Lulu and Mellie walked home together with Charlie and Henry.

They stopped to swing in the little park, all four in a row, which took up all the swings.

"You missed loads when you disappeared this afternoon," Charlie told

Lulu and Mellie, as they swung. "Mrs Holiday trying to read *Harry Potter* and then going mad. Mental maths when nobody knew a single answer. The guinea pig escaping out of the window. The secretary and the biscuit tin. We ate every single biscuit in Mrs Holiday's special tin! She made us do who-can-hold-their-breath-the-longest competitions and gave them out as prizes."

"You missed the park, though," said Mellie cheerfully, swinging so high and so wildly that hair clips tumbled from her hair and were lost in the grass for ever.

"We didn't. Not really. We were there this morning."

"This morning," said Mellie, "was completely different to this afternoon."

This morning, remembered Lulu, *I found my egg. I miss my egg.*

"Better or worse?" demanded Henry. "Which was this afternoon, then? Better or worse?"

Although, thought Lulu, *there are things you can't do with an egg up your jumper.*

"Better or worse?" echoed Charlie.

Lulu waited until her swing reached its furthest point forward, let go, and flew.

"A million times better!" she shouted, and landed in a heap.

"Mad!" said Mellie, scuffing with her toes to make her own swing stop. "Mad! Bonkers! You just shouldn't do it, Lulu!"

"You say that every time!"

"If you're going home now, can I come with you to see the animals?"

"You know you can."

"Can we as well?" asked Charlie.

Lulu nodded.

"The rabbits and the parrot? Snail world and Sam? The hamster and those black and white mice? All of them?"

"All of them, except my duckling," said Lulu. "I keep him in the park!"

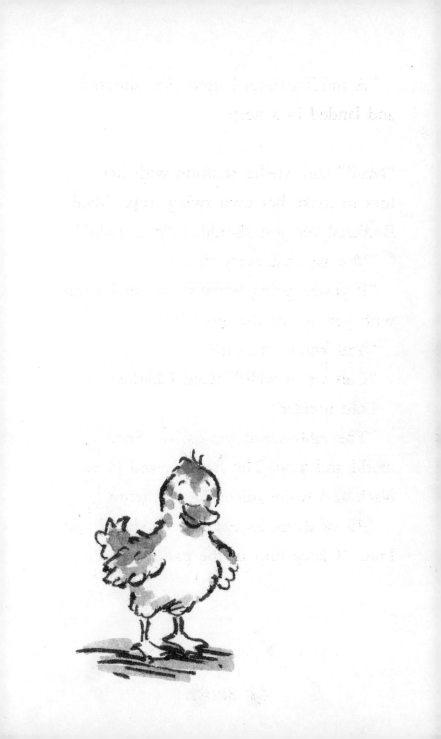

Look out for more

adventures.

COMING SOON!